HOTEL TOLEDO

Melinda B Hipple

Cover art: © Melinda B Hipple
Design & layout: Steven Asmussen
Copyediting: Linda E. Kim

Quitab Editions: an imprint of
Glass Lyre Press, LLC
P.O. Box 2693
Glenview, IL 60025

www.GlassLyrePress.com

HOTEL
TOLEDO

To Jo (Zoe), my first Toledo friend.
She is missed.

CHAPTER ONE

I was born a coward—a fact that, until recently, I had managed to keep quite confidential. This trait has now moved from surreptitious burden to public brand. If I had opened my door just once to allow Dottie inside my boundaries, perhaps she would still be my neighbor. Of course, I can't be sure of that.

From time to time, I would hear the unnerving rattle of someone testing my door. Dottie, pressing her fingers against the knob. I suspected it was Dottie. I never suspected she was trying to break in. She was lonely. The type of lonely that befalls elderly people who have outlived siblings, cousins, friends. She rarely complained. Her feet shuffled down the hall several times a day as she wandered past my apartment door. Quietly, I ignored her curiosity and stuffed a modicum of guilt for my antisocial behavior. When I saw her sitting in a spot of sunshine on the lobby sofa, I would stop and chat. Once or twice a week, I could spare some minutes for a pleasant exchange of useless information. Nevertheless, behind my own hollow-core door—a paper-thin travesty that vibrated the comings and goings of everyone in the hotel and kept out nothing but prying eyes—I wanted anonymity. I guarded my tiny living space with the ferocity of a wounded pit bull. I was afraid of these people. More than that, I feared what it said about me that I lived among these people. I should have opened the door.

It was March, and Sidney lay beside me on the sofa. He raised his eyes toward the ceiling but kept his muzzle resting on his paws. Together, we listened to the dainty footsteps pacing the floor above. A door opened. A voice rose in anger. Marty was home, and Kristine must have forgotten to do something trivial again.

"Good boy," I praised Sidney when he did not growl. "You ignore them better than I do."

Dottie's phone rang. It echoed down the hallway from her half-open door to the marble-floored lobby at the far end of the building. I counted. One ring. Two rings. Dottie's heavy footsteps thumped in the distance. Three rings. She stumbled closer, and I imagined her frail hands testing the walls as she hurried toward her apartment. Four rings. Her orthopedic shoes tromped past my door and kicked her own, slamming it open the rest of the way. At ninety-five, she was surprisingly quick on her feet. Five rings. "Hello?" I tuned out the words.

Amid Dottie's louder-than-necessary half of a conversation and the accusations and apologies raging overhead, I heard the sweet and simple sound of a music box. It was brief. Something on the television? The news anchor's somber tone from behind his desk assured me it was not. The nightly newsman. Dottie. Kristine. Marty. Their voices blended into a jumble of wordplay as the curious, simple sound of a music box played six or seven measures and then stopped. It had to have come from the lumberjack's room.

I called him the lumberjack when, in truth, he simply trimmed trees and underbrush for the Native American settlement nearby. I didn't know his name. He made no attempts to be social, but I could certainly forgive such a failing. I had only seen him twice as I passed his open door. Once, he pushed the borrowed hotel vacuum and had his back to me.

Medium build, sandy-haired. The second time, he stood in the middle of his studio apartment staring at something in his hand. I glanced in and out and kept walking. When you overhear every detail of your neighbor's routine, from when he showers to his favorite television fare, you try not to make eye contact. It was a pretense of privacy. I'm certain he had not been holding a music box.

There I sat in the cold and dreary light of mid-March, caged in the menagerie that was the Hotel Toledo, and wondered what should be so unsettling about the sound of a music box. Sidney raised his head—possibly alert to the music, possibly attuned to the subtle tension in my arm. I soothed his head and neck, and reassured him that it was, again, none of our business.

"Let's take a walk," I said, and he jumped to the floor and cantered to the chair near the door. He sniffed at his leash and looked impatiently from me to it. "You're a good boy. So smart, aren't you?" Sidney bit play-fully at the black nylon strap now hooked to his harness. He stuffed his nose in the crack of the door and waited eagerly for me to pull it open.

In the hall, he tugged toward Dottie's open door while she chatted with a granddaughter about her plans for Easter. I stole a lingering look into her room. With Dottie's poor eyesight, she would never know. Her anonymity was preserved.

Through a series of stolen glances, I came to know Dottie's room intimately. Across the tiny space opposite the door sat a beige-pink sofa frozen in the fifties and preserved with doilies and preciously-gifted hand-made throws. The center cushion allowed just enough room for her to sit amidst a lifetime of memories—scrapbooks stacked to her right, toiletries and a hand mirror trayed on the left. Behind the magazines, she'd propped an ornate plastic mirror. Next to that sat an emerald green glass bowl accumulating light bulbs, new or used. The deep windowsill showcased an array of pungent, half-empty perfumes, cheap but popular in whatever decade they were purchased. A small table sat in front of the sofa. In my neurotic desire to stay detached, I never let my eyes fall on that one tiny patch of living space. I can describe detailed patterns in the overlapping area rugs, the looped texture of the Herculon sofa, even the brick-orange shade of an opened tube of lipstick on the floor. But I never once let my eyes fall on the table top.

Dottie stood beside the table and talked more coherently than any ninety-five-year-old had a right to. Her thick, black shoes held tight against her support stockings. Her black dress—new in the fifties—hung just below her calves. In place of a jacket, she wore a vibrant purple blouse opened in the front and worn through at the elbows. Her painted nails matched the tinge of color at her lips which, in turn, echoed the smeared circles of rouge on each translucent cheek. She wore no eye makeup. Time, and failing health, had etched her lids and under-eyes the color of rust. White lashes fringed her ice-blue irises—a strange counterpoint to an abundance of teased, auburn hair held away from her face by rhine-stone-covered plastic combs.

I tugged at the leash to pull Sidney away from the open door. He obeyed quickly, anxious to do his business in the bushes along the alley-way.

"Good morning, Carl," I said as we headed through the lobby.

Carl looked up from the mop he used to scrub the smell of smoke from the fractured marble floors. The strong odor of bleach mixed with the smell of tobacco and Dottie's talcum.

"Good morning, Mrs. Warner." Carl wheezed through his emphysema as his newest cigarette jumped up and down in his lips. He nodded at Sidney and smiled a little. "Kujo," he said, chuckling at a faded conversation. With some pride and trepidation, he added, "He may be small, but I bet he could lick any dog in this neighborhood."

"Maybe so," I agreed, "but then he trembles at the sight of a black trash bag on the curb." We both laughed, and I moved on past him toward the door.

Carl was afraid of dogs and only tolerated Sidney for the sake of his best tenant. I understood his feeling of unease, for I had the same trepidation about Carl. Accommodating as he was, Carl's temper could flare at the smallest provocation. The first time Sidney growled at him, we almost landed on the street. I patched the misunderstanding by secreting dog treats into Carl's hand at least once a week. The two of them held an uneasy truce. I trusted Sidney's judgment of the man and was wary myself when alone in the lobby.

I pushed through the front door and breathed in the small-town air, clearing the smell of smoke and solvent from my lungs. Sidney raised his own nose, sniffing out the latest information carried on the early spring breeze.

At times, we wandered the neighborhood in search of squirrels. He would scent their trails, or I would spot them in trees and point. Once cornered, the squirrels would flip their tails at the dancing dog straining at his harness. Occasionally, they would creep down the trunk, edge close enough to scold us for being so forward. We walked the alleys and court house lawn, careful not to defile private yards. In the two years we had been living in the hotel, Sidney and I had carved out our own private world in public view.

We turned right and headed south, down the street.

***

I dozed on the couch in front of the television. The usual two a.m. banter between infomercial hosts went silent, replaced by a low-pitched hum punctuated by an occasional tone that sounded hauntingly familiar. I pried my eyes open just enough to let in the light from the television screen. Pong. I closed my eyes and tried to clear my thoughts. Confused, I opened my eyes again, this time concentrating on the picture tube. The screen was black except for a vertical line along each side and one short line drifting back and forth between them. The wandering pixels of light hit the left side and sounded—pong—and then drifted to the right.

"What is that doing on my TV?" I asked in the wee hours. I lifted my head off the pillow and watched the small line bounce back to the left. Cell phone signals. Crossed wiring. I didn't understand it. I didn't care. I simply wanted to go back to sleep.

I pulled the pillow up under my head and tried to empty my mind again. Voices echoed from the lobby. Two, maybe three second-floor tenants were stumbling home from an alcoholic binge. They lingered a bit too long, and Carl soon called from his living quarters as he shooed the loiterers up the staircase. The laughter and footsteps faded slightly. Sidney stood up and shook himself, ringing his dog tags against each other, then circled a half dozen times and settled into his new sleeping position.

Marty must have been among the party animals, because his heavy steps entered the apartment above, and the door slammed shut. For the next thirty minutes, I watched a sideways game of Pong and listened to my upstairs neighbor heaving into the toilet. I remember hearing the two-thirty chime from the courthouse clock.

***

Someone once sent me a quote from one of those endless streams of Internet quotes circling the cosmos. "A person who learns from their mistakes is smart. A person who learns from other people's mistakes is smarter." Perhaps there was something I should be learning from these people.

"Carl!" Dottie's voice cried from the hallway in front of my door. Within seconds, Carl plodded toward our end of the hall.

"Isn't it a little hot in here?" Dottie whined artfully, hoping he would do her bidding.

"Now, Dottie, you know I have to keep it turned up for the tenants in the front of the building. I don't know why you can't open a window." Carl's firm-but-pleasant voice gave away his frustration.

"I don't want flies in my apartment."

"Dottie, it's too cold for the flies to be out."

"Then it's too cold for my window to be open!"

Bells rang out on Family Feud as Dottie and Carl came to the same impasse they reached four or five times as week. I grabbed for a newspaper to stir what little fresh air crept in my own open window. Two floors up, someone's woofers vibrated a trouncing beat down the iron girders that supported the building. Mumbling, Carl headed for the lobby again as the faint sound of a music box played beneath the radiator's mocking hiss. The tune was beautiful. And oddly disturbing. It was so out of place.

The first time I hid from Dottie was by accident. I'd just gotten out of the shower and thought I'd heard tapping at my door. But in the hotel, it was hard to tell whose door and who was doing the tapping. I ignored it. Now there was no question. Dottie needed a collaborator in her struggle to control Carl. I patted the dog to keep him quiet and stayed planted on the couch. I could always say I'd been napping.

Dottie never knocked a second time. In that, she was respectful.

"Carl!"

From the lobby, I heard, "What do you want, Dottie?" Carl no longer hid his aggravation.

I searched for the tiny melody that had captured my attention earlier. Donnie Osmond chatted with the latest Pyramid celebrities as I turned to stone. Dottie must have won out, for an hour later, the room turned chill. Sidney stirred, wanting or needing to be walked. He pranced at the end of his leash as I opened my door. I turned toward the lobby and tugged Sidney forward. Just as we reached the lumberjack's door, Sidney stopped. He stood, hackles up, facing into the room. I could feel, more than hear, his low growl vibrating up the leash. As I caught up to him, Sidney began to bare his teeth.

Inside the room, Lumberjack faced the door while he inspected something shiny in his hand. I reigned in the leash to get better control of Sidney and offered an apology.

"Sidney! Bad dog!"

Lumberjack smiled and said, "No problem." He reached for the door to push it closed just as Sidney lunged forward, stripping the leash through my fingers. I winced as it snapped taught against my wrist. In a rage, the dog snarled and barked furiously at the man's feet. Two more inches and he would have sunk his teeth into Lumberjack's shins. Stepping backward, I dragged Sidney out of the room. As soon as he was clear, the door slammed shut.

I hurried through the lobby, thankful that Carl wasn't sitting at the communal table. Perhaps he was puttering in the basement workshop or, hopefully, he had made his latest run to the Salvation Army Thrift Store to upgrade someone's furniture.

Once outside, I let Sidney sniff at the nearest patch of dried grass while I collected myself. Lumberjack had not flinched at Sidney's affront, but he could still turn us in. Carl needed very little excuse to evict a threatening dog. Though I could stand leaving this emotional abyss, I had no where else to go. I watched Sidney do his business and automatically pulled a plastic bag from my pocket. "No one else would let you in," I cautioned.

"We have to be careful." I would promise to carry my companion in and out of the building. I would watch more carefully for opened doors. I would grovel at Carl's feet and plead Sidney's case.

I deposited the bag in the trash bin and cut the walk short as we retreated to the safety of our apartment.

***

A week passed, and Carl had said nothing. Lumberjack's door remained closed. Other than the dull ache in the pit of my stomach, life was back to normal.

I opened the door for our morning walk and found Carl standing in the hallway. He had a hand on Dottie's doorknob. I had second thoughts about who had been testing my own door and averted my eyes when Carl looked our way.

"Mornin' Kujo," he said as I worried about Sidney's demeanor. The dog simply walked up to Carl and wagged his tail. "I don't have anything for you, Sidney." Carl reached his hands out to show they were empty.

I relaxed my grip on the leash and forced a smile.

Carl pulled a newspaper from his jacket pocket and tried wedging it with the three others that were already pinched in the crack of Dottie's door. "She loves her sports," he said, chuckling under his breath. After a third try, he turned to me. "Have you seen Dottie lately?"

"No," I answered. "Maybe she's at her granddaughter's."

We waited until he had fitted the paper into the crack, and then Sidney and I squeezed past Carl and down the hall. It was one thing to meet him in the lobby, but the stories of his past stint in a Texas prison made close contact in small spaces quite unnerving. It was unfair to judge him,

I knew. As far as I could determine, he'd lived an exemplary life since buying the hotel.

The building was warped and shoddy, though Carl kept it bug free. Several of the walls were resurfaced in cheap material butted against the impressive woodwork and stone masonry of the original craftsmen. Bare fluorescent bulbs washed a sickly green glow across the cement gray paint that concealed intricate oak wainscoting. Once-elegant sleeping rooms had been dissected and recombined into small, awkward apartments paid for by the week. Eighty dollars bought little accommodation. I had taken more than one cold shower. I cooked meals on the only working burner on the stove top. I could asked Carl to replace or repair it, but I was not inclined to invite him in.

Sidney insisted on turning north this particular morning. We walked up the hill and across the street to the courthouse lawn. We paraded around the lush green grasses that surrounded the county offices. An occasional face peered through the office windows and passed judgment on the comings and goings of us "hotel" people. A lawyer stepped from his office door and walked across the street toward the courthouse entrance. He smiled at us. I averted my eyes.

Sidney finished his business and reluctantly let me guide him back toward the hotel. We stepped into the lobby where a new tenant sat at the communal table and talked to Carl in a low voice. As soon as he saw us, he fell silent. Sidney strained to get closer, wanting to sniff out information from the pant legs of the man dressed all in black.

"Kujo," Carl mumbled past his smoking hand.

"Good morning," I said to the man in black and kept Sidney at a safe distance. So far, the dog had not been inclined to judge the stranger at the table. When the new tenant failed to smile or reach toward Sidney in greeting, I pulled at the leash and started toward the hall.

Carl called after me. "Have you seen Gordon around lately?"

I stopped and turned back toward the lobby. "Gordon?"

"Your neighbor."

Ah, the lumberjack. "No," I said, afraid for what might be revealed about our last encounter. I stood like a schoolgirl waiting to be dismissed.

"He's three days overdue on his rent," Carl explained both to me and to the man in black. "That's not unusual for some, but it's not like Gordon. He's always been good bout takin' care a business, if you know what I mean." His manner of speech deteriorated into its colloquial pattern, indicating that he was no longer speaking to me. He reserved his most polite, if not condescending manner, for both Dottie and me—the two older women in residence.

Sidney wagged his tail and smiled a dog's smile as he turned down the hallway toward our sanctuary. When I stopped at my doorway, I noticed a faint smell—something sweet and sour and not quite pleasant. Dottie's door was ajar, but her lights were out. Even in the dim light, I noticed that her sofa had been moved. I unlocked my own door and let Sidney run free into the apartment. Once inside, the smell grew stronger. I walked toward the kitchenette and glanced at the overflowing trash can. It was then I realized that, if not for Sidney and the consumption of food, I had no reason to leave the room I was standing in. I had come to this place to live out my anonymous life in semi-poverty. I could do nothing, be nothing for the rest of my life and never disturb anyone. If the walls didn't fall down around my head, I might still reside here in forty years, wearing the same navy blouse—worn through at the elbows—over the same black pants, my hair coiffed and orange, and demanding that Carl adjust the steam heat on my command. With great effort, I forced myself to bag the trash and carry it through the lobby and around back to the bin in the alley. I lifted the plastic corrugated cover on its hinge and tossed my refuse into the mix. It rolled past a cardboard box covered in reddish brown paint. Someone must have repainted their walls. I was sure Carl wasn't paying for it. When I returned to the kitchen, the smell was still there.

"I should wash the bottom of the can," I murmured to the dog. "Maybe later." I moved to the sofa and clicked on Jeopardy. Dottie's phone rang. No one answered it.

***

May began colder than usual. I shut my windows against the chill, holding in the stale air and magnifying the sweet malodor that pervaded my kitchen. I'd had enough. I pulled the plastic liner from the trashcan and tied it off. The can looked clean enough, but something had to be causing the stench. I walked through the bedroom and into the tiny bathroom shower. No use wasting precious hot water. Cold rain spattered against the side of the can and on to my face and arms. Just as I was about to turn out the excess water, someone pounded at a nearby door. Startled, I dropped the can on the shower floor.

"Gordon! You in there?"

I let my heart settle into a calmer rhythm and waited.

Carl beat harder at the hollow door, shaking the light bulb over my bathroom mirror. "Gordon!" he repeated, obviously angry. "I hear you in there!"

The wad of keys that hung from the retractable ring at Carl's waist rattled, and soon the lumberjack's door swung open. I finished my business and replaced the can in the kitchen. Sidney began to pace the floor, so I snapped on his harness, and we stepped into the hall. Carl was just exiting Lumberjack's apartment.

"God damn it," I heard him mumbling. When he saw me, he apologized. "Well, if Gordon skipped, he didn't take anything with him."

I shrugged my response and squeezed past him toward the lobby where Sidney and I vanished out the door.

***

Spring skipped to summer in less than a week, and soon everyone's windows were thrown open to the hot and humid wind. The sounds that previously had been muted by plaster and glass were magnified off the brick canyon walls of the downtown business district. Marty and Kristine were forced into a temporary truce but, occasionally, I would hear Marty's demeaning insults and Kristine's pouting apologies. They seemed more cautious knowing their biographies were open to the outside world.

"People have walked away, Kristine," I suggested to the ceiling.

Other tenants unknowingly shared their life stories with those us of who listened. I made a distinction between conversations heard through walls and those cast callously out the open windows. The latter seemed fair game.

Sidney begged outdoors more frequently, and in the heat of the apartment, I was inclined to oblige. We would spend a few minutes chatting nonsense with whoever was about on the cool marble floors in the lobby. Most often it was Carl.

When he wasn't working, the newest tenant—the man in black—became a fixture at the communal table. As I walked Sidney through the lobby, I could detect a muted Eastern European accent that hushed as I entered the room. Carl would look up from the conversation and smile at me as I kept moving past them toward the outer doors. I was curious about the man in dark, tailored shirts, but not enough to intrude. As the outer doors closed behind me, I would catch a word or two in thick, broken English. A mystery. The hotel was full of mysteries. Including mine.

"Hey. You hear about the stabbing?" Carl asked in mid May.

I paused, wondering what seedy bar or crumbling neighborhood he might be talking about. Small town, small world. "No," I responded casually.

Carl shook his head. "You know your upstairs neighbors?"

"Oh, no!" I couldn't help but show my surprise and concern. "Is Kristine all right?"

Carl laughed, causing his emphysema to kick up. When he had finished hacking and caught his breath, he explained, "Kristine said she was cooking and Marty was trying to grab the knife like he was playin'. Why, I don't believe that." He watched for my reaction. "She pushed the blade clean down to the bone."

I grimaced.

"You don't do that playin'. There's no way." Carl didn't wait for my response. "I told them to move on out. I don't want nothin' like that happenin' here, accident or no. I mean, I could use the rent, no doubt about it, but that's not so important as havin'," he gasp for air, "a safe place for the likes of you and Dottie to live. Don't you think?"

I was less surprised by the stabbing than Carl imagined I should be. Certainly, I thought a lot about where I lived and why. But I was no better than those I sat in judgment of. What made me different from my neighbors was how they lived their spare lives in the open while I cowered on the sidelines and pretended to be superior. Even Carl provided some service, meager as it was.

I caught my reflection in the Fifties speckled mirror tiles that covered ancient layers of lobby wallpaper. An oval face, with its narrow chin, was accentuated by extra weight around the jowls. Thin lips, unpainted. A narrow nose with a decidedly off-center bump halfway to the bridge rested between almond eyes once complimented by friends and lovers. Hair—boy short, neat, nondescript—carried more salt than pepper. Mine was the costume of obscurity.

"I'm sure Dottie will feel safer," I replied aloud to the ghost in the mirror, "but don't evict them on my account." I smiled at Carl and waded through self-pity toward the hall. "It's time to walk the dog."

I escaped to my rooms and stood frozen just inside the door as my despair drained the remaining color from my cheeks. I wanted to cry, but too much time had passed. Even Dottie, at ninety-five, had more life in her than I could possibly muster at that moment.

And then there was Kristine. The mouse had finally roared. "Good for you," I whispered. "You have a real chance now."

I heard an accusing voice bounce angry words off the alley walls followed by several whimpering apologies. "…medical bills we can't pay and now we're homeless!"

"I'm sorry, Marty. I'm sorry."

I shook my head and collapsed near Sidney. "I'm sorry, too, Kristine." Accident or intended, the mouse was still a mouse. And I was still a ghost. Dottie? The woman who demanded consideration and was not afraid to claim her space in the universe had been silent for much too long, it seemed. I began to worry about my neighbor.

***

It was my birthday. I walked Sidney and gave him an extra treat before locking him in the apartment. With my canvas bag, I walked three blocks to the corner store and picked out a week's worth of rations. Kristine stood at the checkout, paying for Marty's cigarettes. She didn't smoke. I walked up behind her and waited for the clerk to tally her goods and make change. I wanted to tell her how sorry I was, to give her a gem of wisdom that might nudge her toward some self respect. I said nothing.

The air had turned chilly again as it could in late May. I took my time walking back to the hotel. Delayed my penance.

"Mrs. Warner." Carl beckoned me into his office when I entered the lobby. "Have you seen hide ner hair of Dottie in a couple a weeks?"

"No," I told him.

"Somebody slipped her rent under my door, but I ain't seen nothing of her." Carl turned toward his personal quarters as if I'd never been in the room.

I stepped into the lobby and bumped directly up against the man in black. We both stepped back, and I apologized. He said nothing, but simply looked at my feet and waited for me to move out of the way.

I hurried down the hall, all the while throwing puzzle pieces together in my mind. The odd smell that had finally evaporated from my kitchen. The cardboard covered in brown paint in the trash. Dottie's disappearance. I shook off the notion of a dead body in the next apartment. Surely, she was fine. Somewhere. It was none of my affair to keep tabs on an old woman.

Later in the day, I heard Carl moving Lumberjack's things from his vacant apartment. He boxed and hauled the meager possessions to the old nightclub in the basement. I only hoped my new neighbor would be as easy to ignore. Carl would wait a few months and then sell Lumberjack's possessions to cover his lost rent. I would try not to wonder if Dottie was alive or dead and whether Lumberjack or the man in black had had anything to do with her disappearance. I only had one charge. Sidney. And he gave infinitely more than he asked for.

***

His name was Bennie. Short for some Romanian name Americans would never pronounce correctly. He dealt black jack at the local casino. Fitting for the man in black. I pried what information I wanted from Carl. It mattered very little. Bennie had never warmed up to my vacant smile as I walked Sidney past him daily. Carl liked him, but I had to remember my own misgivings about Carl.

Dottie's sports pages hung and disappeared from her doorway again, but I'd not seen nor heard anything of her yet. It seemed odd that in the heat of summer she wasn't leaving her door open to allow for a breeze or fanning herself on the lobby sofa.

I threw the massive window sashes high and put my crock pot away for the summer. Marty and Kristine had moved on. The new girls in the apartment above weighed half as much as their footsteps implied. Young and impulsive, they threw parties on the weekends and played music until three in the morning. With no schedule of my own, I adapted my routine to their sleep patterns. It was easier than complaining to Carl.

The music box played for several measures before I picked it out from the background noise. As the cylinder rotated twice around and plucked its metallic tune into the air, I knew it was no longer in Lumberjack's old apartment.

Sidney came alert and let me know his wish to go out. I obliged him, stopping in the hallway long enough to listen for the compelling tune. Nothing. Sidney insisted on dragging me to the lobby. As anxious as he was for relief, he made time to check the floor under the communal table for crumbs from Carl's breakfast.

"You just missed the food, Sid," Carl said as he came out of the office.

"You spoil him." I realized that Carl's character was no longer an issue for me or the dog.

"Gotta keep Kujo happy," he said, and he reached down to rub Sidney's ears.

We walked into the summer air—shedding the oppressive heat of the hotel—and wandered into the grassy patch between the hotel and the alley. While Sidney sniffed out urban rabbit trails, I looked up at four floors of crumbling brick and mused over the thousand-plus stories the hotel had been privy to. In a time when the marble floors reflected their original opulence and newly fringed velvet dripped from the massive windows, the hotel would have been the social center of the universe in this tiny community. The flock-papered walls held their secrets, for sure, but the intimate lives of the wealthy patrons here would have had some sway over the outside world. The frayed and mismatched curtains that now hung from plastic rods and barely touched the peeling window sills served to hide today's tenants from the rest of humanity. Even in the open air, I could feel the barrier that isolated me from everyone and everything. I hauled poor Sidney inside sooner than he cared to go.

At the end of the hall, Dottie's door was open a foot or so. Sidney sniffed through the crack. I saw Dottie's black-skirted knee protruding from the welted edge of her fifties sofa and noticed the furniture had been restored to its original position—the wooden feet slumping into the old depressions in the carpet. Change was a frightening thing, sometimes.

I wanted to knock and say hello. I wanted to tell her that I thought she had been murdered so we could laugh about it. Instead, I pulled Sidney back and unlocked my door. Inside, I flipped through the handful of television channels until I could decide which innocuous program would require the least amount of thought. Dottie's phone rang. I practiced ignoring her one last time.

***

I began the day like any other. Numb. But in late evening, as I tuned into the TV game shows and social pabulum, my stomach ached ever more than normal. I drilled Alex Trebec's image into my head to erase the look on Dottie's face as they placed a pair of menacing handcuffs on her frail and shriveled wrists. She was barely surprised. I was stunned. She cried like an incorrigible youngster caught playing a naughty prank on a rival neighborhood child. She expressed no remorse, only frustration at the sting of threatened punishment.

At ten a.m., a police officer questioned me as he wrote down my irrelevant facts.

"No I.D.?"

"I don't drive," I said. "I've never had reason to get one."

I overheard conversations in the hall, and this time I strained to listen. Official voices remarked on the crime as they logged each piece of evidence and speculated on how long Lumberjack's body rotted away on the other side of my kitchen wall while Dottie chopped off pieces small enough to wrap in the sports pages that Carl had so dutifully supplied. How could Carl not know? And here I stood—nearer to Dottie's life than anyone, and most ignorant of all.

At ten after ten, Carl appeared wanting solace. "I just can't believe it," he kept repeating as he wandered, uninvited, to my sofa and sat down. Sidney jumped up beside him. Carl paid him no mind as the dog's muzzle rested on his paws and his eyes flirted from me to Carl and back. I could have used Sidney as an excuse to escape outside, but I stood near the bedroom door and watched Carl wrestle with Dottie's stunning deed. "I just don't believe it. Do you? Why would she even do something like that?"

I shrugged and said nothing.

"How could she? Why, I know she's healthy as a horse," Carl continued as he talked his way in circles and tried to explain away his incredulity.

She was old. Too old. She was stubborn beyond belief. Yes, she was strong, but Gordon had to be stronger. He was such a nice guy.

"Can you even believe it?" Carl asked for the tenth time. "Why, even if she was strong enough, ya know," his head shook sideways as he talked, "why on earth would she ever do such a damn thing as this, pardon my language? I've known Dottie for years. She's never even so much as looked crossed-eyed at anyone."

"Dementia?" I asked aloud, grasping at anything to placate Carl.

The strain on his face eased just a bit. It was an excuse he could live with. "Yeah," he said. "Maybe so." For Carl, Dottie was more than a tenant. She was part of a mystique that Carl clung to regarding his precious hotel. He would never have tolerated their quarrels, the games she played, had it not been for Dottie's grande dame status. She represented the glory days of the Hotel Toledo. Without Dottie, the hotel was little more than a collection of rogues, drunkards and shameless personalities.

I tapped at Sidney's leash. On cue, he jumped off the couch and started whining. We escorted Carl to the lobby and escaped out the front door. To Sidney's delight, I kept him outside until I was sure Carl had retreated into his office. Then, carefully, we threaded our way back through the activity that ran the length of the hall and returned to our rooms.

An hour later, a persistent knock forced me to open my door to the glare of a flood light as a faceless cameraman and a clown-faced reporter crammed into the tiny space between Dottie's door and mine.

"How well did you know the accused?" The microphone swung toward me and threatened to dislodge my teeth. "Do you have any idea why Mrs. Rayburn might have wanted to harm Mr. Munson?"

Rayburn. Munson.

"How long have you lived here, uh," she checked her notes, "Mrs. Warner, is it?"

I flushed at such a public mention of my alias.

Inside Dottie's apartment, near the kitchenette, a gloved officer placed something heavy into a plastic evidence bag. Dottie's skillet—the cast iron she lifted every day like a training weight when she cooked her meals. In shameful silence, her grandson Billy sat on the doilied sofa, his head in his hands, obviously trying to get his thoughts around his grandmother's guilt. A uniformed officer scurried past him, tidied up what the police had deemed unimportant.

No longer hiding my curious gaze, I ran my eyes around the familiar room. The cloyingly-sweet perfumes were gone from the windowsill. For the first time I realized the window to the left, tucked behind one end of the sofa, was not a window but a door. The position of the sofa blocked the knob and deadbolt. Through the dust-colored glass, I could just see the top of the dumpster in the back alley.

I began to wonder what else I had missed, and then I saw it. In plain sight of Billy's grief, in the middle of the tiny table that held up Dottie's daily living, sat a silver music box. No one paid it any mind.

Was that it, I asked myself. Was there no better reason to carve the life from someone?

"I have something on the stove," I said and closed the door on the one-eyed cameraman and his mouthpiece.

From the hall, I heard the reporter's voice stab through my paper-thin ego. "Cooking what, I wonder." Her callous and accusing whispers resonated through the door. "She heard and saw nothing? Right. I wonder what her story is."

My story. I was not yet ready to tell it. Perhaps at the age of ninety-five I would no longer care if I was carted off in handcuffs, but on this day, there had been too many revelations. Dottie would certainly lose her freedom. Trapped by my cowardice in a prison of my own making, I had to ask, "Would I know the difference?"

Chapter Two

Hotel Toledo was a hellish place in summer. There were days when I suffered the heat in a tee shirt and shorts only to peel those meager threads off in the dark of night and stretch across the top sheet covering the bed. I stationed a box fan facing outward in the window to push the stale air into the alley while a second fan spilled muggy heat directly across my legs and bare back. Even Sidney could no longer stand to lie beside me. He shifted fitfully from position to position, panting desperately. When I finally dragged myself from bed in late morning, I welcomed the cold showers which were a staple of hotel living.

Fourth of July had come and gone. The police had cleared Dottie's room of evidence and Billy was packing the last of his grandmother's belongings to be stored at his home until the family could distribute keepsakes and mementos. The furniture would stay.

That part of my past that held me here kept threatening to expose itself. There were days when I knew everyone suspected me of something. Admittedly, the hotel tenants now suspected every other tenant on principle. That was Dottie's legacy.

Sidney asked to go out. I pulled on my dirty white sneakers and slipped a bra beneath my shirt. The lobby sat empty as we headed toward the outer doors. Sidney pulled in the direction of the courthouse, but I held him back. Lawyers and clerks doing business in the county offices no longer welcomed us with smiles. Guilt by association. I pulled Sidney toward the back alley.

When we returned to the lobby, Carl sat at the table while he ate his microwaved lunch and read a newspaper. "Hey, Mrs. Warner. Did you read the want ads in the shopper today?"

"No," I admitted and decided to have a seat across from him.

"It's the damdest thing, pardon me," he said with a chuckle and began to read. "'Mystery writer looking for research material.'" Carl breathed a little heavy as he spoke. "'My character needs to get away with a murder. Strictly confidential.'" He rolled his eyes. "Prob'ly cops lookin' to catch some idiots like they do on them giveaway stings they pull ever so often."

I maintained a blank expression.

"I'd send this to Dottie," Carl said, only half joking, "but she really didn't get away with it, now did she?" He screwed his face up and shook his head. "Damn, I still can't believe it."

I glanced at Sidney who lay on his side to take full advantage of the cool marble. He seemed willing to spend more time, so I asked if I could take a look at the shopper. I turned to the front page and took my time wandering through the ads and classifieds. When I stumbled on the mystery writer's request, I read and reread the address. Casually, I slid the paper back to Carl's side of the table and stood to leave.

"I was wondering," I ventured to ask, "do you have anyone interested in Dottie's apartment yet?"

"Well, no actually." Carl's lungs whistled as he drug the air in and out with great effort. "Nobody wants to go the extra ten bucks a week for the separate kitchen. Least, that's what they say. Why? You interested?"

"I think I would be," I said. "I could take Sidney directly out into the alley without worrying who was in the lobby."

Carl raised an eyebrow. "Are you havin' a problem with anyone in particular?"

"No," I assured him. "But if you ever had another tenant with a dog, they wouldn't have to cross paths."

"Why, sure," Carl agreed. "You still have to bring him 'round for his treats, though."

"Certainly," I said. I tugged the reluctant dog up from the marble. "Let me know when it's ready."

"Be ready tonight, if you want."

"Maybe tomorrow." I thanked him and walked back to my room. Once inside, I found a scrap of paper and jotted down the address I had been repeating in my head. I stared at the paper and wondered what to do with it. With no clear idea, I pulled open my purse and tucked it away where it would sit a few days and then be pitched with the garbage. Surely.

Since Dottie's arrest, the nights in the hotel had taken on a different tone. Noises once ignored seemed to scream through the quiet hours. Most tenants were asleep after two a.m., but often I could hear the padding of footsteps toward someone's bathroom or the sound of restless feet as someone tried to out-pace the heat. More often, the noises came from the building itself as it settled a micron at a time into the dirt. When the girls upstairs would tread carelessly, bits of plaster would flake and rain down on top of the suspended ceiling tiles over my head. I stifled the urge to cover my hair.

I gave up sleeping when the sky showed signs of daylight. It was only five a.m., but I had things to do this particular day. Sidney watched me from the bed as I pulled my clothes from the borrowed dresser drawers and stuffed them into a large trash bag. I found a small plastic tub in one corner of the closet and gathered my toiletries into it. It seemed strange to pack for such a short move. As quickly as I could box the handful of items I used each day—shampoo, soap, a comb, toilet paper—I could walk them into the new bathroom. In the kitchen, I added a handful of eating utensils and the few pantry items.

Five-thirty. Too early to wake Carl. I sat on the sofa and clicked on the television. "…four easy payments…you'll never have to scrub again…cut your cooking time in half…" I clicked the television off again.

A weight heavier than I could bear descended around me. I was half Dottie's age, and yet I felt so very old. I looked around the shoddy rented room at the worn rented furniture next to the rusting rented appliances. In the middle of the sloping floor, a small plastic tub and a black trash bag held everything I could claim as my own. No Billy waited to parcel out my mementos. I had no mementos. Even Lumberjack had owned a music box. It suddenly mattered to me who would get the shiny stolen treasure. I had said nothing, and now the ornate silver box was destined to pass down through the wrong family.

My thoughts shifted from the music box to a hand-blown glass bowl, beautifully elegant and rich with color. The bowl represented my own bloody secret, and it made me laugh. I laughed so hard my eyes began to water. Sidney came in from the bedroom and sat beside me on the couch while my laughter turned to sobs and then again to howls of amusement. My shoulders shook hard with the release of emotion. Soon I was spent and laying sideways on the cushions. Sidney licked my fingers, tasting the salt tears I'd wiped from my face.

I fell back to sleep by the time Carl knocked at my door.

"Mrs. Warner? You need any help movin'?"

I cracked the door a few inches and assured him that I didn't.

"Here's the new keys. Just get me the old ones when yer done."

I thanked him and closed the door again. I wiped down the sinks and counters—not that anyone could tell much difference—and made a last check of the rooms before stepping across the hall. Sidney wandered straight into Dottie's living room, glad to finally satisfy his curiosity about the place.

"This is your new home, Sidney." I glanced at the beige pink sofa and made a mental note never to buy a doily. The dog started to lift his leg in an effort to claim his new territory, but I scolded him just in time. "We don't pee where we sleep. Remember that."

The living area was larger than my previous one. The windows to the alley sat lower in the wall and provided a better view of the world.

"Don't buy doilies, and don't walk around naked."

Sidney stopped to glance at me and then headed off again.

Across the room, an opening with abandoned hinges and striker plate led into a tiny kitchen. The cabinets were layered in dirty gold paint that showed hints of two previous colors. I could sand and paint them easily enough if I wanted to spend the money. The counter tops and stove were in reasonably good shape. I could see now that I would reap the benefits of Dottie's demanding personality.

Right of the kitchen was a closed door leading to what had to be the bedroom and bath. I turned the knob and pushed the door open. Sidney ran ahead, thrilled at the thought of having adventures without his leash. He stopped inside the door and sniffed at the carpet. When he didn't move out of the way, I reached around to flip on the overhead fixture. The dark, paneled walls sucked up most of the light, and I waited for my eyes to register the new surroundings. Sidney began to dig at the carpet with his teeth. I shooed him the rest of the way into the room.

"Stop that!" I chastised him. "I'll feed you soon enough. You don't have to eat…" I froze in awe and disgust. Sidney turned back to the carpet and continued to sniff at the perimeter of a large stain. The color of rust paint on cardboard. I saw Lumberjack's broken head spilling out his life while Dottie teetered on her heavy black shoes as she gripped a skillet in one hand and touched the wall for support with the other. Any hint of morbid curiosity I might have had was soon swept away by waves of nausea. I ran to the bathroom and fumbled for a light switch. Thanks to Dottie's stubborn will, the fixtures in the bathroom looked new. This distracted me enough to get control over my rebellious stomach. I leaned into the sink and waited until the nausea had passed. When Sidney pawed at the stained carpet again, I ordered him to stop.

The face in the mirror sported a number of scars. Some were physical, healed over and no longer painful. Others were emotional, half buried but still raw to the touch. My eyes were dull—tired and puffy from my early morning sob fest. I contemplated asking for my old rooms back. Once again, I found myself the victim of bad choices and resigned that I would stay. This was where I belonged—halfway between the living and the dead.

Penance comes in all flavors. Mine was to live in a tired hotel in a room that carried the pall of death. For the first few days, I used the alley door exclusively to take Sidney outside. I couldn't face anyone, especially not Carl who would be watching me curiously. I lived out of the trash bag, refusing to put my clothes into the dresser in the bedroom. I laid a towel over the stain and only walked over it on my way to the restroom. I slept on the sofa, but that was not unusual. I watched television. Obsessively, I cleaned the kitchen.

By the end of that week, I was down to a can of tuna and a box of crackers. I showered and changed into my last set of clean clothes and quietly locked Sidney in the room. When I was reasonably certain no one was about, I walked through the hotel and into the glare of the summer sun. The quiet of the street marked a lull in the town's activity.

At the local market, I selected my usual rations. While digging for change, I found a stray piece of paper with an address on it. I stared at it a moment and then poked it back into a side pocket. I finished paying and stepped outside. When the light on the corner turned green, I turned right instead of left and walked to the courthouse lawn. Comfortable that no one was paying me any mind, I sat on a bench and slipped the paper from my purse again. I folded and unfolded the scrap several times. My inner voice argued that responding to the ad was as idiotic as Carl knew it to be. I should have tossed it in the trash, but something about Dottie's recent escapade lit a spark inside my coward's heart. Even Kristine's brief attempt to assert herself shamed me.

I stood up from the bench and walked back across the street and past the market. A block and a half more stood the newly-renovated town library. I slipped inside.

The exterior doors opened into a large, echoing lobby. At the far end, near a second set of doors to the library proper, was a large glass case. I stopped at the case to gather my courage and to practice my sideways glances. Just inside the main library entrance, on the right, was the check-out desk occupied by only one librarian. Directly in front of her were a handful of computer stations, some of them populated. I stared back at the display in front of me as I pretended to read placards about a butter lady famous for sculpting farm animals out of milk fat. The sculptures were quite good, actually. Just buttery.

After staring dumbly at the grainy photos for several minutes, I pulled open the second door. Eyes ahead, I marched past the librarian's desk and into the newly-constructed wooden stacks. The smell of construction glue and cut lumber permeated row after row of alternating classics or new releases. I turned left down the center aisle and found a row that kept me safely out of view of the woman fussing over the latest returns.

"Now what?" I ventured to ask the many plastic-covered book titles. I pulled a few books off the shelf and pretended to leaf through them or read the jacket reviews. I turned down another row and caught sight of the computer stations again. Too many people. I toyed with the idea of checking out a book before remembering my status as a nobody. I replaced the book in my hand and walked back toward the exit. Near the desk, the librarian looked up from her chores.

"Can I help you find anything?"

"No thank you," I said and kept moving—past the desk, through the double doors, past the butter cow lady and, at last, to freedom. My knees shook the entire walk back to the hotel. I chastised myself for playing into my fear and yet delighted in the energy it created. I felt more alive than I had in years. I knew then that I would have to write the letter. No matter what.

***

The last week of July set new heat records. Sidney and I walked in early morning and late evening, but during the horrid heat of midday, I left him in front of the fan and escaped to the library to spend time in the air conditioning. My fourth day there, I found the computer stations unattended. I sat down at the one that gave me the clearest view of the room. It had been a while, but I found my way into a word processing program. Before I could type a word, a motherly voice said, "You need to sign in to use the computers."

Startled, I looked up at the librarian who, I was sure, had not been behind the desk just moments before.

"I was just looking for a website," I explained, surprised at how meek my voice sounded.

She smiled generously and said, "That's no problem. We just ask that anyone using the computers sign in and note the time. We keep track in case it gets busy so everyone can have a fair turn." She pointed toward a clipboard.

I stood and walked toward the counter. When I picked up the pen, I realized that I had no full name to give her. For almost two years, I had been Mrs. Warner. Carl did not require a written lease and had never asked my first name. Worried that I had hesitated too long, I looked further up the list and found a name that would suit my purposes. I quickly scribbled Mary Warner and logged in the time. The librarian motioned me back toward the computer.

"I'm Zoe, if I can be of any help." Her smile was genuine, but her eyes were clouded with sadness, perhaps weariness. For the first time, I noticed her hair. Thin and weak. Chemo, most likely. I wanted to ask and perhaps offer sympathy, but I didn't want to intrude. I never wanted to intrude. I simply walked back to the computer and sat down.

After familiarizing myself with the different options, I settled on a font and began to type, *Dear Mystery Writer.* I stared at the screen for another few minutes before continuing. *I'm writing in response to your want ad. I have knowledge of a crime that was committed some years ago.* I read the last sentence through a few times and then backspaced and rewrote, *I have certain knowledge that I would be willing to share. What kind of information do you think would be most helpful?*

I could have told my story then and been done with it. I knew the risks, but something in me craved the interaction. I added, *I do so enjoy reading the shopper. Yours truly, Anonymous Research Assistant.* I leaned back and stared at the words on screen. The act of writing the note, even unsent, changed me at that moment. This mystery writer, anonymous as a priest, would hear my confession and, perhaps then, I could take back my life. When Zoe was free, I walked up to the counter.

"How can I print off a letter I've written?"

Zoe started out from behind her desk.

I panicked. "No, I mean, I know how," I said quickly, "but where does it print out?"

"Oh." Zoe turned back to the desk. "Just hit print, and I'll hand it to you."

"Okay." I turned away before she could see my cheeks flush.

At the computer, I opened the letter again and wondered if I should hit the delete button. Surely, Zoe wouldn't dare read the page right in front of me. What did it say after all? Nothing incriminating. I held my breath and clicked print.

I emptied the word processor of what I'd written and closed it down. At the counter, I waited for the hum of the machine to stop. Zoe reached for the page and handed it over without a glance. Just as quickly, I folded it in half and tucked it into my purse. I thanked her, paid her a dime for the copy and walked as casually as I could from the library back to the hotel.

Sidney didn't get up but simply greeted me with a sideways thump of his tail. I stripped off my street clothes and pulled on a tee shirt and shorts. Before I could settle on the sofa and open my purse, someone knocked at the door.

"Mrs. Warner?" Carl called in his rasping voice.

"Just a minute," I answered and threw an oxford shirt over my tee. When I opened the door, Carl stood holding my Crock Pot.

"You left this in the other apartment. You still want it, right?"

"Oh, yes," I said, taking the slow cooker from his hands. "Thank you."

"Yeah, well, a new guy moved in last night and he found it in the cupboards. A Mr. Varble. Retired fella I think."

"I'm glad you could rent it out so quickly."

"Well, seems all the apartments go pretty quick." He drew in a long breath and grimaced at the effort. "'Cept this one. I appreciate you makin' the move. How's it working out?"

"It's good," I told him. To change the subject, I asked, "How often does the County Shopper come out?"

Carl coughed twice and sucked in air. "Once a week. On Wednesdays. We got a new one up front if you want a look at it."

"No, thank you anyway. I was just getting ready for a nap. But don't throw them away when you're done with them." I started to close the door.

"You lookin' for work?"

The question caught me off guard. There were only three reasons to read the shopper—to buy something, to sell something, or to look for work. Four if you counted the personals. "I was thinking I might check around," I said casually. "Not that I need the money."

"The casino's always hirin'. Maybe you could check out there."

"I'll look into it. Thanks again." This time I managed to get the door closed before another word was spoken. I hurried to the sofa and retrieved the letter from my purse. *I have certain knowledge* it read in pica ten-point type.

Sidney rolled over to cool his other side in front of the fan while I stared, unblinking, out the windows and into the treetops until the images of separate trees fused into one jittery mass of green and blue. "Was I sure?" I asked myself, but I knew the answer. My only question now was where to mail the letter from. Not the hotel, certainly, and not from Toledo. Maybe the casino? I would need envelopes and stamps.

A few minutes later I heard an unsettling rattle at my door. I waited for someone to knock, but whoever was in the hall did not announce himself. When everything was silent again, I quietly opened my door. Something fell to the floor. At my feet lay the County Shopper.

***

Sidney walked into an uncut patch of grass and began pulling up the blades with his teeth. After he'd plucked a mouthful, he patiently waited for the greens to settle his stomach.

"I understand, buddy," I told him, feeling queasy in the unrelenting August heat. When he moved again, I followed his lead.

It had been two weeks since I'd taken one of the infinite number of tour buses that ferried gamblers to and from Ames, Iowa. I began my journey by walking to a local motel and waiting for a free shuttle that catered to the casino patrons. My intent had been to post the letter from there, but it required handing the envelope over to a desk clerk, and still the letter would have been postmarked from Toledo. Instead, I waited at the curb and stepped onto the next charter bus heading west.

I don't remember the parking lot in Ames where the driver pulled to a stop. My mind was cued to the free-standing mailbox on the sidewalk a few yards away. I slipped off the bus with the departing passengers, walked casually to the box, and dropped the letter through the slot. Just as casually, I walked to the end of the line of new passengers waiting to board. In two days time some literary wanna-be would slice the envelope open and perhaps find something of interest. I would dutifully read through the papers that Carl now fitted regularly into the crack of my door.

Sidney walked to a patch of grass between the sidewalk and the street and lay down. I let him rest for a moment or two and then tugged him to his feet. "Time to go, buddy." We took our time climbing the slight slope of the hotel grounds toward the front door.

Inside, Carl read the bi-weekly town paper which snapped back and forth each time he rattled out a cough.

"Good morning, Carl."

"Hey, Mrs. Warner. Hey, Sidney." Carl reached down to scratch the dog behind the ears while I pulled out a chair and sat down. "You had any luck with a job?" he asked me.

"Not really. I'm not sure if I want to work. I don't really need the money."

Carl pulled his upper body back in his chair. Even this slight move created an obvious strain on his face. He laid his smoking hand on the table and watched a stream of nicotine rise in a column from the burning leaf. "I been meanin' to ask you, if it's not pryin', just where you get yer money. You retired already?" He leaned in again and took a short drag from his cigarette. "You ain't old enough to be collectin' Social Security, are ya?"

I said nothing about my inability to claim what would be rightfully mine someday. Instead, I glanced down at Sidney asleep on the pitted marble tiles. We sat in silence for a while, staring at the dog or the paper or out the lobby doors.

Over the next few days, I left Sidney alone more than I should have. He suffered in the oppressive heat of the hotel while I retreated to the cool recesses of the library's reading nooks. As an apology, I managed to bring him a small treat each afternoon.

Zoe worked most days. When she was alone behind the desk, I would linger a bit and ask about a particular book I'd picked from the shelf. She seemed eager to chat, and yet her manner was restrained.

One Wednesday afternoon, I walked in to see a bald-headed woman leaning over a stack of newly-returned books. I hoped the flush on my face would be taken as a reaction to the late August heat. Perhaps it was, or perhaps Zoe had grown accustomed to the awkward reactions from library patrons and people she passed on the streets. I could pretend all was normal, or I could mention the obvious. Something in me was tired of pretending.

"Zoe. All formality aside, and if it's not prying, may I asked how you are doing?" To my relief, she relaxed her posture and leaned a little more in my direction.

"Pretty good, really. My doctor says the tumors have stabilized. They're not shrinking, but they're not growing either." She described the latest round of treatments and what might be next. She finished the conversation as though we'd been talking about her health for months. Her words, her tone of voice filled the moment with hope, but the shadow never lifted from her eyes. Life for Zoe was in a terrible limbo. To some small degree, I knew how that felt.

I walked home to find the County Shopper skillfully wedged into the crack of my door. Inside, Sidney stood anxious and hungry. After a brief walk, I made him sit for his supper, and then I curled onto the sofa and began scouring the columns of ads in the personals section. Halfway down the page, I found what I was looking for.

"Anonymous Research Assistant: What evidence was destroyed and how? My character needs a clean get away! Confidentially, MW."

As I read the words, my mind raced ahead to the many possible conclusions to this daring distraction. So far, I had done nothing to jeopardize my anonymity. Why should I tamper with my current state of affairs? I looked around the tiny, sterile room with its shoddy paneling and exposed piping. I laid the paper off to one side and began to compose my response. Details. He wanted details. It would require dredging up some very painful memories, but I was committed to excising my ghosts. My confessor would hear it all.

***

At three in the morning, the television scrambled to snow, and I started awake on the couch. I flipped channels to find that they were all dancing with static. The first breath of cool air I'd felt in weeks wandered in through the open window. Along with the breeze came the smell of garbage. Sidney looked up from the floor.

"I guess I've worn the poor thing out," I said, rubbing his ears briefly. I clicked the off button, and the room went dark.

Someone above dropped their feet to the floor and padded toward a restroom. Private noises filtered through the plaster and timber, and then the footsteps retreated again. Soon, there was a mind-numbing silence about the place.

By nine a.m., I had not moved, nor had I gone back to sleep. My eyes traced the edges of several stains in the ceiling tiles and counted the number of nails that had been used to secure the sagging squares. Carl's resources were limited by the caliber of tenant he could attract which, in turn, was restricted by the ambiance of the rooms, which, inevitably, came back to the quality of repairs done over the years. Still, for an ex con, he carried his own weight.

At one minute after nine, I sat up. Sidney raised an eyebrow in my direction to see if I would move toward the kitchen. When I didn't, he simply wet his nose and closed his eyes again.

I reached for my purse and pulled up the lining where I'd torn it loose many months before. Inside, I retrieved some of the money stashed there. Fanning the bills, I made a mental note of how I would use them in the next few days. Four crisp hundreds would cover a month's rent and buy food for both Sidney and I. The last bill, precious for the freedom it represented, would pay my way to another distant mail box. It was a lot to risk in both money and security.

After Sidney had been walked and fed, I headed straight to the library. Zoe was not about. I signed in using my alias and sat at my usual console. I opened two programs, minimizing one that I could retrieve if someone came too close. Alone in the corner, I set to work typing in the details I had tortured over in the early morning hours. The letter would have to be worded carefully to keep the authorities off my trail if this brazen author did turn out to be a hoax.

Dear Mystery Writer,

First, I must tell you that this was a crime of passion, and though the killer was never jailed, he or she has suffered greatly over the years for what they have done.

For the sake of storytelling, I will say that the killer was a man. The victim, a woman. No charges were ever filed because no body was found. The man claimed the woman had simply run off, and authorities could find no evidence of foul play in the home.

Let's just say the argument was over money. There had never been any violence between them, although, in the last few months they were together, they argued frequently.

The night in question was a holiday. The killer had just bought the woman a gift of little value—an afterthought rather than a display of affection. This began an argument that lasted several hours. While the accusations were flying, the woman accused the man of having no ambition. He slapped her. She hit back. In the ensuing struggle, he grabbed the nearest object and hit her on the head.

This is where the killer's luck becomes a major player. Lucky for him, anyway. The blunt object was a paperweight he had made in his studio. He was a glass blower.

There was little blood from the wound and only a small amount on the globe. Most of the hemorrhaging appeared to be internal. The killer quickly placed a trash bag between the woman's head and the carpet where she'd fallen. He took the globe to the garage and placed it in with his glass stock. He fired up the furnace and returned to the kitchen. Under the sink, he located a pair of rubber gloves and put them on.

His second stroke of luck was the unfinished barbeque pit in the yard. The couple had exchanged many cross words over the fact that the hole had been dug months before but was filling with leaves and debris. Sacks of concrete and mortar sat beside pallets of unused brick.

Returning to the living room, the killer wrapped the victim's head in the bag and carried her to the trench. He carefully scooped the dead leaves to one side and, after laying her in, covered her with dirt and more leaves.

His next order of business was to fabricate a reason for her disappearance. A computer-generated suicide note or letter of goodbye would hardly fool her relatives. He located the personal journal she kept in her dresser and thumbed through the pages. On several pages he found lengthy essays about her desire to leave him. He chose one that sounded particularly like a goodbye letter and cut it from the journal, folding it into a small envelope.

Next, the killer systematically collected clothing and several of the woman's favorite things. In the garage, he cut her suitcase into small pieces and patiently fed them into the now-hot furnace. He burned her clothes, underwear, shoes—anything that she might have taken with her. Finally, he tossed the journal into the inferno.

He washed his hands in the utility sink, scrubbing with bleach and soap.

Returning to the furnace, he grabbed a gathering ball and collected a scoop of glass and the paperweight and fed them into the heat. The blood on the paperweight was quickly burned away. When all the pieces had merged into a pool of molten glass, he reached his blow pipe into the fires. Carefully he puffed and spun the glass—stretching its shape. When he had finished the piece, he cut it from the pipe and placed it in the cooling kiln.

The only remaining evidence was a collection of jewelry that he eventually melted and used to decorate the edge of the exquisite glass bowl.

When all the other evidence was cleared away, he rolled a wheel barrow from the garage to the debris-filled grave site. With the garden hose close by, he mixed and poured barrow after barrow of concrete into the hole until he'd filled and troweled a base for the final layer of brick and mortar which he finished two days later.

The police investigated after the victim's mother had reported her missing. The killer showed them the note and let them search the house. They questioned him several times about her disappearance, but he was never charged.

Though the case was never solved, know that the killer lives in his own private hell.

Yours truly, Your Humble Research Assistant.

I sat back in the chair and reread the letter only once. I was afraid that, if I began editing, I would lose the courage to send it. I hit the print button.

Chapter Three

It was mid-September. The heat let up, promising a pleasant Fall, but I had difficulty sleeping. Without the television's masking noise, I heard every snap of timber, every footstep, every joyous or cross word spoken anywhere in the building. I listened intently to who came in and out of the lobby, waited for some cold, official voice to question Carl on the whereabouts of the women in this picture. Afraid of my own shadow, I closeted myself in my room and tried to think of some way out of my little melodrama. When I could stand it no more, I slipped out through my personal exit and headed for the library.

Zoe greeted me with a warm smile and a full head of short, thick hair.

"Wow!" I said, unable to stop myself. "You look great. How is the treatment going?"

"Good," she said with a dismissive smile. "I haven't seen you in a while."

"I've been busy." After a long pause, I asked, "Anything new I should be reading?"

"Yes, actually. I'd recommend *Peace Like a River*. I just finished it, and it's really good." She headed into the stacks as I followed. When she pulled the book and placed it in my hands, she said, "Why don't you get a library card so you can take this with you?"

I turned the book over a couple of times. "I can't," I admitted. "I don't have I.D."

"Nothing with your picture on it?"

After years of isolation, I let Zoe into my space. "None that I can share with you."

She raised an eyebrow and then nodded to reassure me that she would pry no further.

"Besides," I said with a weak laugh, "it's cooler here."

Zoe walked me over to my usual reading chair and left me to digest my own thoughts. After fighting the first few lines of the book, I was soon swept up in a story of violence, family ties and the supernatural nature of God's love. What seemed like only moments later, Zoe tapped me on the shoulder and told me the library was closing. I slipped a small scrap of paper into my place, returned the book to the shelf and left for the hotel.

I braved the lobby to find Carl smoking and sipping a soda in his usual spot at the communal table. "Hey there, Mrs. W," he said, chuckling at his own cleverness. "I haven't seen you and Sid around much lately. Everything all right?"

I sat across from him and leaned onto the table top. "I've been a little under the weather. I'm feeling better now."

Carl looked concerned. "Well, now, you just let me know if there's ever anything you need from the store like medicine or somethin'." A vague look of melancholy flashed across his face. "I used to get stuff for Dottie all the time. She was a pistol." He shook his head. "Thing is, I miss the livin' daylights out of her."

I envied Carl. He had someone to care about and who, even from prison, must have cared about him. It struck me then, the happenstance that prison was something he and Dottie now had in common.

"Have you heard from Dottie? How is she doing?"

Carl looked eager to answer. "I went to see her the other day. Got permission and drove all the way to Oakdale." He saw my blank expression. "They got a medical unit there. Prob'ly put her there 'cause she's so old, and all." He smiled a little and said with some admiration, "She was lookin' pretty good for being in such a place. They must be treatin' her pretty well."

"I'm glad to hear that," I said for his sake. I shook off the recurring image of Lumberjack's broken head forever laying on what was now my bedroom floor. "Has Dottie ever said why she did it?"

"Nope," Carl stated sharply. "I even asked her that. She just looks kinda dazed and says 'What's past is past.' Even Billy can't get nothin' out of her. I'm just hopin' she lives comfortable in whatever time she's got left. Prison can be pretty hard on anybody." He lowered his eyes.

I looked at Carl's face and wondered how many years of hard labor were etched there. The gray in his hair extended into his two-day-old beard and even into the flesh that hung from his sunken cheekbones. I had blamed cigarettes for his poor health, but perhaps they were only part of the story. "Carl?"

"Yeah?" he said, looking up from his moment of introspection.

"Could you find me a really cheap television?" I watched his eyes light up a bit.

"Sure. I can probably pick somethin' up next time I'm at the Goodwill. They usually have a few. How much you want to spend?"

I shrugged. "Can I get something for less than thirty dollars? It doesn't have to be much."

Carl's shoulders straightened. "Thirty bucks, I can get you something pretty good. I'm going up Thursday. That soon enough?"

"Plenty," I said and gave him an appreciative smile.

I excused myself from the table and headed down the hall to take Sidney for his walk. As soon as I had him harnessed and stepped into the hall, the door to my old apartment flew open and an elderly man, eyes glaring, stood silent in the doorway.

"You must be Mr. Varble," I ventured.

Sidney pulled forward toward the familiar space. As soon as he reached the threshold, Mr. Varble kicked at Sidney, lifting the dog slightly off the ground and sending him backward. In a rage, Sidney scrambled to his feet and went after the aggressor. A second kick sent Sidney yelping against the door jam. By then, I had reeled in the leash to get Sidney out of harm's way. I picked him up and held him tightly in my arms, trying to control his thrashing as he attempted to strike again at the evil thing before us.

Carl appeared in the hallway and started hammering us with questions while Mr. Varble and I stood our ground at arm's length.

"What happened?! What's going on here?"

Sidney's barking echoed furiously in the corridor.

Never taking his eyes off me, Mr. Varble said, "Her dog tried to bite me."

"Only after you kicked him!" I shouted back, holding onto his stare with equal intensity. Sidney had quit struggling, but he continued to bark into the man's face.

Mr. Varble sneered at me and turned his head toward Carl. "I want that dog out of here."

Flustered, Carl's eyes batted nervously as he shook his head. "Now, wait a minute," he said, trying to calm us both. Looking at me, he asked again, "What happened?"

I looked directly at Carl and said in my calmest voice, "Sidney walked over to the doorway of his old apartment and that man kicked him."

Mr. Varble never countered my claim or tried to offer another explanation. He simply repeated, "I want that dog out of here."

Carl was obviously torn. I could see he believed me, but I also knew how desperate he was for the money his tenants provided. I thanked my lucky stars that he had never found out about Sidney's reaction to Lumberjack. Two such incidences, no matter how provoked this last one was, would surely have landed us on the street. Carl lowered his head while his right hand picked nervously at his scruffy tee shirt. "Okay," he finally said. "Mrs. Warner, could you possibly take Sidney out the back from now on?"

I wanted to stand my ground, but in fairness to Carl, I nodded agreement.

"And you, Mr. Varble." Carl avoided direct eye contact as he said, "I'm not sayin' you was wrong, but I've known Mrs. Warner a long time now, and in all her dealings with me, I've never known her to lie."

I could not stop the blood that rushed to my face.

Mr. Varble did not protest the implied accusation against him. He simply stepped back into his apartment, mumbled "I hate dogs," and slammed the door in our faces.

Carl looked at me and shrugged.

I lowered Sidney to the floor and let my shoulders sag. "I promise you, Carl. Sidney did nothing wrong."

"I believe you," Carl said in his quietest voice, perhaps not aware of how futile it was to whisper in such a place. "Don't you worry," he assured me. "I'm not throwin' you and Sid out for the likes of him." He thumbed at the closed door. "You and Sid are welcome here for the rest of your days, far as I'm concerned."

I know Carl meant his last statement as a comfort.

***

Sidney was in no mood to walk one Thursday morning. The suffocating summer heat had returned for one last stand against autumn, and all he could do was wander, listless, along the edge of the sidewalk next to the hotel. I stepped into the grass and tugged at the leash to encourage him. When that did not work, I picked him up bodily and deposited him a few feet into the grass. "Poop," I commanded in a quiet voice. He only managed to snap at a fly buzzing near his head.

When Sidney decided to lay down in the shade, I took my cue and sat on the grass beside him. I'd been picking at some wild violets for a while before I noticed a dark face staring from the shadows of our old apartment. Mr. Varble was watching us through the high window. I held his gaze for a very long time. When he became uncomfortable, or simply grew tired of standing, he moved back out of sight. I reached over and scratched behind Sidney's ears. "Let's go, buddy," I said, climbing to my feet. "I'll bring you out again later."

We wandered back through our private door. Sidney took his spot in front of the box fan, and I stood in the middle of the room staring at the cavernous hole that led to the bedroom. I don't know if it was Mr. Varble's treachery, Zoe's kindness, or Mystery Writer's query, but something broke the lock on my spirit.

"This is my home now," I exclaimed to Lumberjack's ghost. Sidney didn't even turn an eye in my direction.

I forced myself into the bedroom to rearrange furniture and put my spare things away in the drawers. I made an internal commitment to rent a shampooer and see how much of the blood stain I could remove from the carpet. After a couple of hours of vigorous polishing, I decided to take a break and cool off in the library.

Zoe was alone behind the desk. She smiled at me when I came through the doors.

"How are you?" I asked.

"Good," she said in a noncommittal way.

That answer was no longer enough. "How is the treatment going?"

Without moving a muscle, Zoe seemed to retreat from where she was sitting. It struck me then that her full head of hair no longer signaled health. It meant resignation. I tried to stifle the mercy that came pouring out, but to no avail.

"Zoe, I'm so so sorry. Is there nothing they can do? Is there anything I can do?" How arrogant, I realized after I'd asked the last question, as if my life had some bearing on hers. My selfish life. But Zoe had the answer.

"Just be my friend," she said. "I could use a good friend." She motioned for me to come behind the counter and sit with her a while. We talked mostly small talk. I asked about her family. She had no one to speak of. "The spinster librarian," she joked.

When she asked about my family, I hesitated. "I was married once."

"Well." She folded her hands in her lap. "Here we are then." After a brief moment of silence we both laughed hysterically. When we quieted enough to speak again, she said, "I cheated on a homework assignment in the seventh grade."

I smiled and countered, "I used to eat the candy in a store where I worked as a teenager."

Her eyes twinkled as she told me, "When I was twenty-four, I stole a highway caution sign. I felt so guilty, I returned it the next night."

She was giving me permission. Zoe would never ask me straight, but she wanted me to know that I had her confidence. It seemed so natural to say it.

"My name is not Mary Warner."

She didn't flinch. She didn't even lose her smile.

"And I'm not divorced."

Before I could say anything more, the spell was broken by two children who came racing through the double doors, heading for the young adult book section.

Zoe greeted them and then turned back to me. "I should get to work." She pulled a list from her work pile and laid it in front of her. "Come see me tomorrow before school gets out."

I said I would and then walked back to the hotel, all the while wondering how far I could trust her with the truth.

Inside the apartment, I found Sidney pacing the floor. There was evidence he had been sick. I hurried to put the harness on and managed to get him outside where he was sick again. He paced, almost running at times, and then he would stop to vomit. I felt sorry and irritated at the same time. He stopped moving long enough to have a terrible bout of diarrhea. At that point he simply laid down in the grass and started pulling at the tender green with his teeth.

"I'm so sorry, buddy." I offered to rub his head and neck, but he growled at me—something he'd never done before. "I'm sorry," I said again and pulled my hand away. He looked at me with the queerest expression, let out a yelp followed by several whimpers and then simply lay over on his side, panting. Shaking. Nothing I could do would coax him to his feet. I was afraid to pick him up.

I tied the leash to a nearby bush and ran to the front of the hotel.

"Carl, I need your help! It's Sidney. He's really sick. Could you drive us to a vet?" I led Carl out of the lobby and toward the lawn. Sidney lay where I'd left him.

"Can you get him up?"

I reached one hand for Sidney's muzzle and clamped his mouth while I ran my other hand under his chest to lift him. He screeched in pain, but I managed to gather him into my arms. Carl untangled the leash just as I looked up at the window of my old apartment to find Mr. Varble's wretched face staring back at us. He was smiling.

***

I am heartbroken to this day. How can I possibly express what Sidney meant to me at that point in my life. He was my companion, confidant, protector. He never questioned my integrity, and he never asked for more than I could give him. For a week, I mourned alone in my apartment. Carl would come by each morning to ask if there was anything he could do. I would send him away. I bawled like a baby, exhausting myself, only to start again the next day.

I found myself shooting daggerous stares toward my old apartment. Fortunately for Mr. Varble, we never managed to open our doors at the same time. He had poisoned Sidney, and I had absolutely no proof. Even if I had, I could never have accused him publicly.

I made myself get out of bed the following Friday. I showered and changed, and before I realized exactly where I was headed, I found myself walking into the library. Someone new stood behind the desk.

"Is Zoe here?"

She looked at me with an odd expression. "Are you family?"

"No," I said.

"Is there something I can help you with?"

"No," I repeated rather abruptly. "I came to see Zoe."

She took my rude response and returned it in kind. "Zoe no longer works here."

Still too dense or too grief-stricken to understand what she was not telling me, I started to ask why when the head librarian stepped out of the back office.

"Mary," she said, smiling at me. "How are you?"

"Not good," I complained. "I really wanted to speak to Zoe. When will she be back?"

Her smile lingered a little too long. "She's not coming back. She's in the hospital."

"No," I said reflexively. "She can't be. I need to see her."

I must have seemed pitiful to the two of them. Drab, sullen, selfish. When I finally came out of my stupor enough to think, I asked, "Where is she? Can I go see her?"

The librarian hesitated only a moment. "I'm sure Zoe would want you to know. She's at the university hospital in Iowa City." She leaned onto the desk and wrote something on a slip of paper. "These are her room and telephone numbers. I'm sure she'd appreciate a visit from you." It was less a statement than an appeal.

I thanked her and wandered back into the street. "What can I do with these?" I thought, staring at the numbers, but I knew I had to go. I had to tell her the whole truth.

Over the next two days, I borrowed Carl's phone to gather information on bus routes. When Monday arrived, I awoke early, still fighting the feeling that I should take Sidney for his early morning walk.

I showered and pulled on my drab uniform of black slacks and casual top, and started my walk to the nearest motel. From there, I shuttled to the casino, the Des Moines bus station and along the stretch of Highway 80 that took me to Iowa City. It was eleven-thirty when a taxi picked me up for the final leg to the university hospital. I made a mental note, calculating how much of my precious resources would be spent on this trip, and just as quickly chastised myself for thinking that it mattered.

As I stepped through the rotating door and into the lobby, the crisp October air gave way to a mix of odd medicinal smells that permeate every medical facility. In contrast, the lobby was full of people shopping, visiting, snacking on light lunches. At the information desk, I asked for directions to Zoe's room. After a couple of false starts, I managed to find the correct wing of the correct floor. Outside her room, I glanced at my empty hands and felt ashamed that I had not brought a card. It would have been an empty gesture, but a gesture nonetheless. How could I have fallen so far from the compassionate, caring person I used to be? I no longer recognized anything honorable within me. And still I pushed forward into the room.

Zoe, a tiny woman to begin with, seemed insignificant amid the countless machines, tubes and wires that traveled to and from her shrunken body. In just over a week, her face had pulled into her skull leaving large hollows under her cheekbones. Her thick short hair matted to her head. She saw me, and immediately, the corners of her mouth tipped up just a little.

"Come in, come in," she ordered with a weak motion of her hand. She patted the bed and whispered, "Come sit here."

I walked to her bedside, careful not to touch anything attached to her or a monitor, and sat gingerly on the side of the mattress.

"I'm fine," she replied to my silent question. With a tiny shrug she added, "It's my lot in life this round." She drew in a deep breath to recover her voice and asked, "What's your name?"

"Rebecca," I said without hesitation. "Becca, to my friends."

"Becca." Zoe rolled the name over as if to inspect it for the truth. "That suits you better."

I dropped my eyes to my hands and fidgeted with their emptiness. After a long silence, I looked at her and said, "I'm so sorry you are going through this. I'm so sorry...." She reached for my hands to stop me.

"I've made my peace. I think it's time you made yours." She slipped her fingers into mine and gave a firm squeeze. "Tell me, Becca, what brought you here."

I couldn't stop myself. I told her everything from Dottie's misdeed and my complacency, to how I had deceived Carl. I laid out the story of Mystery Writer and recited word for word what I'd written in the letters, how I'd laid out the crime scene in detail.

"You cannot imagine what it was like," I said, "to wake from the struggle only to be suffocating in blackness." I was sorry as soon as I had said it. Zoe could imagine.

"Go on," she prompted.

My body shuddered, fighting the memory. "I ripped the trash bag away from my face and lay gasping under a layer of leaves and dirt. For a while, I couldn't remember my own name. I crawled out of the pit and hid behind the studio. I watched for hours as my husband worked to hide what he thought was a murder. At first, I was only stunned, but then I grew angry. I tried to imagine what the police would do to him if I reported the assault." My eyes flared with a darkness that surprised even me. "He was good at talking people out of things. At worst, he would receive a shorter sentence than I was sure he deserved."

I stopped talking and looked at Zoe's serene expression. "Perhaps you can't understand this, but I could think of nothing greater than the hell I could heap upon him as a ghost." I turned away for a moment. "The truth," I said, turning back, "is that I was afraid to face him. Too cowardly to confront him with what he'd done. Too afraid I would forgive him. And so," I said, raising my hands into the air, "Becca vanished."

Zoe watched with pity in her eyes. "You saved yourself," she told me then. "There's nothing disgraceful in that." She looked tired, fighting to keep her eyes open.

"I'm sorry," I blurted. "I'm wearing you down."

"Nonsense," she admonished. Again she grabbed my hand. "Thank you."

I couldn't hide my surprise. "For what?"

"For trusting me."

When I knew my time with her was over, I said, "Your turn to tell a secret."

A low moan escaped her throat. "I loved a married man once." She paused for effect. "And then he divorced me." Still she clung to humor. "I should rest now. I'll see you soon."

I leaned in to hug her frail shoulders. "Yes," I repeated. "See you soon."

We both knew we were lying.

***

I fell into a dark depression over the next two months. My limited existence became even more constrained as my reasons for escaping the hotel had now all disappeared. Carl kept a close eye, and when he realized that I had not been out of my apartment in over two weeks, he offered to buy groceries. I let him.

I heard him rattling plastic bags on his return from the store. He tapped lightly, and I pulled myself up from the couch to open the door.

"Here's yer things," he said, handing me two small sacks. "I put yer change in the one with the orange juice." When his right hand was free, he removed the cigarette from the corner of his mouth and used the butt of his hand to cover a phlegmy cough. "You jus' let me know if yer needin' anything else."

I held the bags open and stared at the contents. Without looking up, I asked, "Do you want to come in for a moment?"

"Why, sure. You must be pretty lonely in here without Sidney."

I backed away to give him room to enter.

"I still can't believe someone would poison a innocent dog like that." He gravely shook his head and walked to one end of the couch.

I put the groceries away in the kitchen and returned to the overstuffed chair that Dottie had used only as a repository for magazines and news-papers. I turned from a vision of blood-soaked newsprint to the sight of Carl's smoking hand shaking steadily as he pulled his cigarette to and from his lips. I sat quietly and watched the gray plumes create patterns in the air around his head. He looked uncomfortable, but I couldn't bring myself to start the conversation.

"So," he ventured after another thirty seconds had passed. "Did you want to git another dog? Ya know I wouldn't mind, if that's what you want."

"I don't know," I murmured. "I honestly haven't thought about it."

"Well, I wouldn't mind, ya know."

"Thank you. I'll let you know before I do."

After another minute of silence, Carl pulled forward on the seat. Before he could stand, I stopped him with a question. "Why were you in prison?"

He raised his eyebrows and relaxed back into the couch. "Most people are afraid to ask. Me, I don't mind talkin' about it. I made mistakes, but who hadn't?"

I nodded. "How bad was it?"

"Bad enough. I was on the edge, ya know. I'd git in fights, or git a little drunk now and then. I did a little petty thievin', but never got caught for that." He looked genuinely remorseful. "No, I got time for knockin' a fella so hard he lost an eye. I used to have a pretty bad temper."

I laughed out loud, but Carl didn't appear to take offense.

He continued. "I only did two 'n a half years the first time, but it hit me pretty bad. I was use to a hard bunch on the outside, but nothin' like what was living inside."

It seemed he'd been waiting, perhaps for years, to tell his story. I needed to spend some time outside myself, and so I encouraged him.

He rambled on for another ten minutes, explaining the reasons why they kept sending him back into confinement. "That was when I finally figured out how dumb I was," he concluded. "I figured it was time to straighten up. Git something ligit goin'."

We were silent again, but this time neither one of us felt the need to rush through it.

"Remember you asked me about my money," I said and watched him perk up with interest. "I won it from the casino."

"Well, I'll be damned," he said. "That's how I got the money for this place. Cost me sixty grand, and I've been losin' money ever since. Why the last assessment they said it was only worth forty-seven thousand dollars. And this being a historical building and all."

"I'm sorry," I told him. "I know how hard you work to keep it up."

"Well, I do what I can."

For a moment he looked uneasy, and then a resolve came over him. "I know things have been rough for ya the last couple a months, Dottie, but you shouldn't let things get you down like this." He seemed oblivious to the fact that he'd gotten my name wrong. "Take it from me. I know about this stuff."

Just as quickly as it began, his lecture was over. He slid to the front of the sofa again. "Well, I'd best get back to that work or things'll fall apart for sure. I'll be firin' up the boiler in another two weeks." He stood up and looked for a place to get rid of his cigarette butt. Finding nowhere to drop it, he took it with him to the door. "It'd be best if you'd get another dog."

I nodded and said I would consider it.

Carl let himself out.

I realized then that my entire life had been devoted to searching out people who would tell me what to do. My husband had been the consummate expert in what was right for me. I bowed to his will because I had no direction of my own. With no one to guide me, my last few years living in the hotel had simply been inertia at rest. How selfish of me to have laid that burden on others.

The flat light from the bare bulbs washed over Dottie's living room, and I noted the handful of past receipts written in Carl's illegible hand and made out to Mrs. Warner. Nothing here had been mine. Ever.

From Carl's private rooms off the lobby, I heard him coughing up his afternoon phlegm to make room for a little oxygen. I could picture the cigarette jerking in his right hand.

It was late when I finally opened my apartment door to the cavernous hallway. I stood staring at the number fourteen that graced the door to my old apartment and wondered if I had the nerve to pound on it until Mr. Varble was obliged to open it and meet my wrath. Instead, I turned toward the lobby. With some regret, I stepped out of the Hotel Toledo for the last time.

Chapter Four

It was, perhaps, the most frightening thing I'd ever done, leaving Toledo. Every other major change in my life had been forced upon me. This was my choice. All I knew for certain was that I had to escape the hotel and Carl and Dottie's legacy. There was one additional thing to break free of, and I couldn't do it in Iowa.

The ticket master in Ottumwa explained the boarding process and motioned to the row of hard plastic chairs along the glassed wall of the train station.

"The Number Nine train is coming in late and will be the first to pull in. Don't get on the first train," he said firmly, fatherly. "About ten minutes after it leaves, the Number Six will pull in. It's waitin' out of town right now. You wanna get on the Number Six." He shooed me toward the chairs.

I sat two seats away from a young woman, perhaps college age, who seemed engrossed in a book. I tried to glance at the title in case it was something we had in common. A conversation starter. When it didn't look familiar, I let my eyes wander to the rest of the interior.

The 1970's architecture had been cared for only slightly better than Carl's hotel. Just a train depot at one time, the space now doubled as the bus station. Two bus passengers waited on the opposite wall and stared at us through the invisible barrier that separated the classes. One man wore everything he owned layered on as if the temperature was sub zero. The other man teased me with his eyes and his body language, threatening to slide across the room and strike up a conversation. He could sense my discomfort. I caught his smile just before I looked away. Lucky money was the only thing that put me on this side of the room.

A last-minute couple, tickets waving, raced in with their luggage and managed to catch the Number Nine. As quickly as the noise had settled into the corners again, the Number Six pulled in from the opposite direction. I followed the college girl and her cumbersome luggage into the night air. The echoing whispers inside the building were absorbed into the humid, small-city noise. A porter checked our destinations and sent us to separate train cars. I was sad to sever whatever imaginary connection I'd built with the young woman.

On the train, I turned left up the spiral staircase to the seating deck. There were two empty seats right behind the bulkhead, and I settled into the one nearest the window. With my purse tucked under my elbow, I waited for the train to deliver me back into the fire.

All night, the train struggled along the track, sometimes jerking to a stop for no apparent reason only to start rolling forward again without announcement. The low interior lights overwhelmed the moonlit land-scapes, hiding everything but the mercury vapors standing sentry over the sleepy farmhouses. The passenger cars swayed precariously with the jointed rhythm of the rails. I felt a world apart from everything I'd known in my life. I wanted to ride trains forever.

It took nine hours for the previous three years to be erased. At four-thirty in the morning, I disembarked at the McCook depot in Nebraska. It was a relief to be the only one there.

A dim light shown from inside the station, so I wandered in to get my bearings. The building was much older and architecturally more interesting than the one in Ottumwa, but the inside was sterile, the ticket counter barred and locked. One table and a handful of scattered chairs barely broke the monotony of the room. The bathroom was clean enough, but there was no lock on the door. I remembered where I was and relaxed into the business at hand.

At the table, I pondered every conceivable outcome of my visit. I listened to my breathing echo through the cavernous room and wondered if anyone was still looking for me. Had anyone in this town ever known me enough to remember who I was? What would they do if they saw me? What would he do?

When dawn finally broke across the tracks, I stepped out of the station and turned toward the business district. Within a few blocks, I was puffing up a steep hill covered in middle-class bungalows. The terrain leveled on a high plateau, and soon I passed the small community college that helped to drive the town's economy.

"He taught here," I reminded myself. I had hated the school functions—him parading his eccentricities before his raptured students, academics speaking snob-ese to one another. Me, the mousy wife in the corner attending the punch bowl. I had never been intellectual enough to suit him. What I lacked in intellect he lacked in ambition. I supposed that made us even.

I passed the college and turned down what used to be a crumbling private drive. There were houses, now, crowding the pasture behind them. Five new modest homes spilled into the tangled underbrush that had once separated us from the city limits. I passed the graveled driveways and wondered if anyone was watching this early-morning interloper. At the end of the pavement, I stopped near a stand of young black locust.

It was still early—perhaps only five-thirty or six. The morning was November cool, but the dry air never stirred. I studied the house and marveled at how little had changed, how it sat frozen in the same state of disrepair. No better, no worse than when I'd left it. The only things new were the swaths of eddied leaves strung across an unused patio surrounding a barbeque pit. My gravesite. I leaned into the small tree trunks and waited for something to happen.

He appeared in the window. He walked up from the shadow of the living room and stood drinking a morning cup of coffee. His hair was longer, to his shoulders, and hung in the same disheveled fashion that labeled him a non-conformist. He held his cup with both hands and watched a half dozen starlings play in the yard. He turned, responding to someone, and I saw him smile. I knew she would be young. Perhaps a graduate student, perhaps not. Of course she would be pretty. She stepped to the window and, from behind, threaded her arms under his. They stared out the window, and together they stared right through me. Drab and gray as the bark of the locust, I was truly a ghost.

When they disappeared into the shadows again, I sank to my knees. Hugging my purse into my belly, I leaned over, rocking and humming my torment. I was a broken woman again. He knew himself to be a murderer, and yet everything I'd done, everything I had not been for the last three years had served up no reprisals. My only achievement was to free him to build whatever life he chose. I was too humiliated to be angry.

I wanted to call to someone, conjure a name that would bring me comfort. I felt a phantom warmth against the side of my leg. "Sidney," I blurted, reaching into the leaves to stroke his fur.

The garage door to the studio lurched open, and I scrambled back into the brush. It wouldn't do for him to find me in this state—a pitiful specter.

He lit the furnace and prepared his tools for a morning of glass work. He checked his blowpipes, blocks and paddles in the same ritualistic way he'd done for years, sorted through his powders and sands, felt each texture a moment longer than necessary. It was his rite before he began casting the ingredients into the fire.

I thought of Dottie and how she had murdered Lumberjack, dissecting his body to dispose of it. My husband was guilty of assault, but it was I who had committed this murder. In my quest for revenge, I had dissected my life into worthless pieces that could be tossed as easily into the fire.

I watched him for hours, turning, shaping, blowing life into inert sand. I wondered what had happened to my bowl. The bowl. Perhaps he had destroyed it, melted it back into innumerable other creations. For a moment, it mattered.

The sun reached midday. A number of new vases—vibrant and sensual—cooled in the annealer. The studio stood empty, heat billowing out the open door.

I got up from the ground and brushed the leaves from my pantlegs. Picking my way through the bushes, I moved to the street and turned away from my past. Through town, past the campus, past the cottages, without intent, I found myself in the train station again. The ticket counter was open.

"May I help you?"

I could return to safety—to the hotel and obscurity—or I could reincarnate from the ashes. There would always be that chance I'd be discovered, perhaps even prosecuted for something. But people endure prison.

"Ma'am," the ticket salesman repeated. "May I help you?"

Sidney was gone. The few belongings left in the hotel—clothes, dishes, television, a slow cooker—could be replaced for less than one of the bills I hid at the bottom of my purse. Everything I was stood passively in this one spot.

"How cliché," I finally said.

"Pardon?"

"Phoenix. Phoenix, Arizona."

"Baggage check?" he asked, looking at my feet.

"No," I said. "No more baggage."